Tales of Dragons

FOLKTALES FROM AROUND THE WORLD

TABLE OF CONTENTS

INTRODUCTION

Have you ever seen something that sent chills down your spine and made you feel just how tiny we humans are? Once, long ago, our world was greater, grander, more magical: it was populated by dragons. These beings were — or are — the essence of wonder, of the amazement we feel towards the infinitely powerful and dangerous.

In this book series, we visit the most diverse cultures from all over the world and delve into the rich treasure chest of their storytelling. The traditional tales in this volume speak of the awesome and marvelous, of the perilous and exhilarating. We shall explore the traditional, age-old stories our ancestors have told us about dragons.

These tales of awe have grown and flourished all over the globe, though, as you travel East, it's likely you'll find more dragons — and kindlier ones. For not all dragons are the same: not really siblings to each other, they're more like removed cousins.

Some are imbued with fire, others with light, others with rain and river water. Some have horns and wings. Others have lion heads, four limbs, and fur. You can find the oddest combinations! This wild variety isn't limited to appearance, though— you'll find dragons both friendly and hostile, selfish and most generous.

But, whatever else they are, they are always majestic. There is no one more stunning and formidable than them. I believe that dragons, however different they may look from us, are the symbol of that part of ourselves that is high and breathtaking. The part of the human spirit that always soars higher than everyday troubles. That within us that longs to fly free over the world, and to conquer it, and to rule it.

Dragons teach us something crucial: we must find and face the great, dark mysteries of our soul. We have to confront the dangers we hold in our own being. Only then will we become worthy of the kingly power of the dragon.

They teach and inspire us, by pitting our heroes against impossible quests, to become the amazing, strong beings we truly are.

An onion and a Lindworm

Scandinavia

Once upon a time, in a remote corner of the North, there lived a king and a queen, much beloved by their subjects, but childless. Despite a good marriage and their strong wish to have a son or daughter, they had almost lost all faith in being able to conceive.

On a particularly lonely winter day, the Queen decided she could not live this way anymore. She wanted— needed— a baby or she would die of grief. Distraught, she went off into the dark and perilous forest, though what she wanted, she knew not. She realised she had lost her way but, before she could be afraid, she saw an old Crone, looking at her from the shadows— with kindness.

'Dear Queen,' the old woman said, 'I see that you are set upon this course. So you will not die, I will show you how to have a child. You must do exactly as I bid and not disobey me, or terrible things will happen.' The Crone gave the Queen one huge, red onion and told her to peel it perfectly before eating.

Doubtful but filled with new hope, the Queen rushed home and, in her hurry to see if the Crone's words were true, forgot to peel the red onion before eating it. 'No matter,' she thought, 'if I have a child, everything else is trifling.' And, true enough, nine months later, the joyous couple announced the birth of a child.

The whole kingdom rejoiced greatly, but the sovereigns were troubled — they had an unsettling secret: the child that had been born was no child at all! It was covered in red and black scales, had fiery serpent eyes, two sharp claws, and a long tail! Fearful for the life of their infant, they built a secure, secluded chamber for him to grow up in. They brought him cattle and he would eat it raw. He grew and grew into a horrible monster, and it was now clear — the Queen, because of her haste and disobedience, had given birth to a lindworm!

The lindworm infant became a child, then a youth, and was, always, alone and friendless. The people were, still, blissfully unaware of the dreadful, dragonish nature of their Prince. So, when the King and Queen, uncomfortable but determined to keep the traditions, announced their son was seeking a wife, the nobles and important families were delighted to send their daughters as potential brides. When the maidens arrived in the castle, dressed

Tales of Dragons

in all their finery and looking as beautiful as ever, the King would take them to meet the Prince, who also said he was keen to be married.

However, once they entered the isolated bedchamber of the Lindworm Prince, he snatched them up, one by one, and devoured them whole. This happened, again and again, and the families had no news of their daughters. No one wanted to send a maiden to the castle anymore, and the Lindworm Prince threatened to escape and eat them all by force. Desperate, the royal couple sent far and wide for a new, brave bride. No one came.

When all hope was lost and the Prince was about to set out on a course of devastation, there came a piece of news. A young woman, a beautiful but poor shepherdess, had come. She told the worried Queen to be still — she had spoken to an old woman who, pleased with her bravery in keeping the sheep, had told her what to do. She was wearing seven dresses — her whole dowry — all at once and was carrying a bowl of milk.

So she went into the frightful chamber and when she saw the Lindworm, she didn't flinch. He snarled that she should take off her dress so he could eat her without trouble, and his eyes were fiery slits. 'On one condition,' she said, 'That when I take off one dress, you take off one of yours.' 'Deal,' the Lindworm Prince agreed, wild with hunger. The shepherdess took off the first layer of clothing and, forced by his own word to comply, he shed one layer of skin, just like a serpent.

'Off. Another one,' he said. But he was already weaker from the shedding. As the maiden took off the dresses she wore, one by one, the dragon sloughed off one layer of skin after another. With each dress she took off, the shepherdess was unharmed, but the lindworm grew weaker: it isn't easy to take off your skin. When the maiden was down to the last dress, the Prince no longer thought of eating her: he was in excruciating pain, even as he agonizingly discarded his last layer of dragon skin. The girl watched, surprised, as there, in a dead faint, lay a bleeding Prince — a human prince! — on the chamber's floor.

She rushed to his side and, with the milk the Crone had told her to bring, she bathed the wounds of the former Lindworm. He, having shed off all the layers of scaly dragon skin (just like an onion), was cured. The King and Queen rejoiced. The two young people loved each other, and the Prince had, finally, found someone who challenged and bettered him to become, instead of a monstrous Lindworm, a good man.

THE GREAT MASTER AND THE RAINBOW

Benin

L ong before man walked on the earth and fished in the streams, before even the oldest of the animal bones lived and breathed, there was Nothing. No planets, no starry night sky, no rocks underfoot — nothing.

In the great Void, there was only the primeval serpent Damballa, a loa (god) of immeasurable power. He was the root from which all the worlds sprouted. How did this happen? Well, Damballa saw that there was nothing around him and did not want it to be so. But there was nothing he could use to create the world — only...

Damballa considered his own body, the only thing that existed. He was strong, and big, and awesome (if anyone had been able to see him, they would've agreed): he could do this!

Using the power and incredible length of the 7,000 coils of his body, Damballa curled and stretched and took shape. He danced a serpentine, dragonish dance until everything was the way he wanted. In this way, the Great Dragon Master created the whole cosmos: the stars suspended in the sky, the uncountable planets, the highs and lows of every valley and hill on Earth, the bones of every mountain. By shedding his skin, he completed his work— his shining, flowing scales became the water we drink, present in every spring, ocean, and waterfall.

After this great task, he was tired and felt lonely. Though he had created the world by himself, he couldn't take care of it on his own. But, when the waters he had made rose from the ground and fell again as the rain, he saw he was no longer truly alone — he saw her. Ayida-Hwedo, the green dragon serpent that is also the rainbow. And she was the beauty.

Damballa, happier even than when he'd created the brilliant gems in the core of the earth, took her as a wife. He tasked her, his beloved, with holding up the skies and filling the waters of the earth with the whisper of amazement.

Through the ages, the love of Damballa and Ayida-Hwedo, the two dragons that are the Masters of the world, has endured. In every child that is born, we can see the fruits of their love, for mankind sprang out of it. And in every corner of the world we see and the air we breathe, the two Great Dragons continue their primeval dance of creation and entrancement.

Tales of Dragons

SHORT-TAILED OLD LI

China

In the poorest of the South Eastern provinces, a farmer's wife (whose name was Li) was in labor. Her husband was out working in the fields, as they were very poor and could not afford to be idle, not even for something as important as birth. The land was dry, desertic, and miserable.

It was hard. There was no midwife to help the poor woman push— she had to guess and do everything by herself. But she loved this baby and was determined to do right, whatever it cost. She labored from sunrise until sundown and, with the last, terrible push, was exhausted. She felt the baby crawling up to her breast— odd. Her tired thoughts couldn't focus on why that was strange though. As she felt the baby start to suckle— sharp teeth?—, she dozed off.

That was how the husband, returning from the field, found them: his wife, lying spent on the bed. And an odd, serpentine shape attached at her breast. He was horrified — that ugly thing could not be his baby!

Full of dread, fear for his wife's life, and sinister thoughts, the farmer grabbed a spade that was in the corner and swung it at the little serpent. A screech. A severed tail. The baby creature opened wings it didn't know it and escaped, with a shower of sparks, out of the window — just as the mother opened her eyes and tried, in vain, to catch her son.

Many sad moons passed between the now lonely and estranged couple. As the middle of May came around, with the anniversary of that terrible day, something odd began to happen. Rains came. Monsoons. Awe-striking thunderstorms that fertilised the land, making it flourish and give fruit like it never had before. And, on the thirteenth of the month, he came.

It was their son! Only, now, he was full grown: a huge, majestic, kindly dragon. He had flown to the far north and, divine as he was (even with a short tail), had become the god of a rich river. Now, he said, he had come back to visit his mother, the one who loved him despite his appearance.

And, though he disregarded his father, he went back to visit her — bringing fortune, fertility, and good luck — every year. He still did, even after her death, to honour her memory. He had become Short-Tail Old Li (just as she was also Li), the dragon that brings rain and abundance, every lunar year, because of a mother's love.

TWO HORSES AND ONE ZMEJ

Serbia

The youngest son of an Emperor fell in love with an enchanted princess that, every night, stole a magic fruit from his father's garden. Their love was tested when his older brothers found out and cut off a strand of the maiden's hair. After giving the youngest prince a longing look, she flew away in the form of a peahen.

As love always prevails, he found her after a long and arduous journey and, of course, they were married with much joy and became Emperor and Empress of a wide realm. But the castle where they lived their love was ancient and held many dark secrets. 'Don't go into the twelfth cellar, not for anything in the world,' she warned.

But one day, after the Empress had just set out on a journey, the young Emperor (of course!) went down to the cellar and a casket asked him for water. One, two, three times. The man thought it was strange, but it was rude to refuse water. Suddenly, after the third time, the casket exploded!

Out of the million fragments came crawling a zmej, an age-old, evil, winged dragon, made stronger and more fierce by its long forced confinement. It was wicked, incredibly powerful, and would not stop until it got revenge on its captors (who had put it in the casket as punishment for its wrongdoings). The Emperor understood this and knew that, even as the zmej flew off, he had little time to rescue his wife.

He found her before the dragon did. Together, they rode upon one horse, without knowing where they went— only escaping. They could feel the zmej chasing them but it had assumed human form and was following hard on another horse. But though human in form, the zmej was dragonish in weight, and the poor mare it rode on was very, very tired.

'I can't go on!' it said to the zmej, 'You weigh too much, you won't let me eat or drink— I will die of exhaustion!' The mare was of the mind that whatever revenge the zmej wanted against the Empress and her husband was, certainly, not as important as the life of the mare herself. But she was forced to gallop onwards. herself. But she was forced to gallop onwards.

Tales of Dragons

Because of the magical power of dragonkind, the zmej and its steed reached the Empress and Emperor, who were riding on their own tired— but very wise— horse. This horse had belonged to a witch and, having learned everything there is to know about dragons and other monsters, he knew exactly what to say to the zmej's poor mare. 'He's killing you, don't you see?' the Emperor's horse exclaimed, 'It's a zmej, of course he doesn't care if you live or die— all their kind are so big and majestic that they only think of their own power and vengeance plots. Our lives are nothing to them!'

The mare, already panting hard, saw the truth in the words of the Emperor's horse and, stopping with a jolt, threw the human body of the zmej down, breaking its neck and ending its wicked life. The Emperor and Empress returned to the castle and lived happily ever after. And thus, the wise and humble defeated the evil and powerful, and love reigned overall.

Y Ddraig Goch

Wales

In earlier times, Great Britain was a lot more forests than in the later days. The cover of trees was so thick on the land that a squirrel could have hopped from the South to the North without ever touching the ground. And, in the vast thickness of the woods, many things lived that are, now, unknown.

One such thing was dragons. No one will ever know the shapes, temperaments and sizes of the many dragons that once lived in the Welsh wildlands, since no one was ever brave enough to go meet them. However, the tale of the most famous among them will always be remembered.

Llud, the Briton King of Wales, was worried. He knew that his land wasn't really his, but belonged to itself and to the many creatures that inhabited it. But he considered himself responsible for the safety and happiness of everyone in it. And, lately, a dragon had been causing problems. It was big, winged, red and, while that in itself was harmless, its screams were making the cattle die and the plants dry out in the ground. Why? It seemed like it was being attacked by a white dragon, come from over the sea, that wanted to kill it.

The King was at a loss. A human, even if he was a King, should not get mixed up in dragon battles. But he had to do something, so he went to his brother Llefelys, who was known to be extremely wise, for advice.

'Brother,' Llefelys replied, 'here is what you must do to protect your people. Follow my instructions faithfully'. He told Llud to dig a well in the very heart of his kingdom— one large enough to hold both beasts inside—, to fill it with mead (dragons are, as everyone knows, great lovers of mead), and to act fast. Llefelys gave Llud a magic cloth. The King nodded and promised to do as he was ordered.

After digging and filling the well with mead, Llud waited out of sight. Soon enough, the two endlessly fighting dragons appeared, biting and tearing at each other. When they saw the mead, however, they folded their wings and rushed to drink. They drank so much that they became quite drowsy and, having emptied the well, they forgot all about fighting and laid down to sleep.

Llud and his men sprang into action! They covered the beasts with the magic cloth and a large slab of white stone, so they would continue to sleep and their devastation would be over.

Someone, though, made a prophecy: there would be a chief who would inadvertently build a castle on top of the dragons' resting place and set them free again. That day, Y Ddraig Goch (the Red Dragon) would kill the white one and set his British land free, once and for all.

THE NAGA DOWRY

Cambodia

O nce, the land at the southernmost tip of Orient was a large and powerful empire. The people were proud, hard-working and imaginative. They built many great temples out of stone and, though they are, today, covered by moss and silence, their ancient glory remains. The secret of the Cambodian people, they said, was in who their ancestors were— or, rather, what they were.

Before any humans came to live in the region, this was the kingdom of the Nagas. Varied in shape and size, the Nagas are all powerful beyond our imagination: they are magical, almost divine beings. Magical shapeshifters, they can alternate between their human and their dragon bodies at will, and, as Kings and Queens of the Underworld, they rule over all its precious gems and treasures. In many occasions, they have ruled over humans, befriended them, or— as in this case— even married them

One night, an Indian Brahmin prince named Preah Thong had a dream. In it, an aged sage commanded him to sail East, towards the Sun, and to act with faith, honesty, and love. Now, the lands in the East were not uninhabited, but ruled by an old Naga King called Sdech Neak, benevolent but wily, as Nagas are wont to be.

Preah Thong set sail and, with hope in his heart, arrived at a small island. It was as far East as he could make it on his own, and he was tired. Leaning against a tree, he slept for three full days and, waking by the light of a midnight moon, saw the most wondrous sight. It was the loveliest maiden he had ever seen! Her movements were like the water, and her skin seemed to reflect the moonlight with an enchanting glow of its own. Unable to help himself, he approached her and, when their eyes met, they fell inevitably, irrevocably in love.

'O human,' she said, 'This is strange! Never have I seen a man as handsome and kindly as you, and yet I am a Naga, Neang Neak, the daughter of Sdech Neak, the King. We are not supposed to marry.' But, as their hearts were already joined, she decided to face her father in his Underwater Kingdom. Neang Neak commanded the prince to hold onto her silver clothing, and they descended swiftly, through wave and coral reef.

Tales of Dragons

The Dragon King, surprisingly, said nothing about the oddness of the match and married them: it was willed by fate. But, after some time in the Underwater Kingdom of the Nagas, Preah Thong got very sick. However ill and pale he got, though, he refused to leave his Naga bride, because he loved her more than his own life.

Seeing this, the Naga King smiled a shrewd grin— his daughter's suitor had passed the test. Of course, a human prince couldn't live underwater! Now wholeheartedly approving of the match, the Naga King gave his daughter, the Dragon Princess Neang Neak, a rich dowry: he used his magic powers to suck all the water from around the island on which the couple met and let it be joined to the mainland.

This land, imbued with the gifts of the Nagas, became abundant, fertile, and prosperous. Of the union of the prince Preah Thong and Neang Neak, the Naga princess, came the inhabitants of the empire of Cambodia, whose descendants are alive today, perpetually embodying the union of the human and the magical.

Tales of Dragons

For a bag of rice

Japan

Fujiwara no Hidesato was the young son of a famous warrior who lived in a town by a river. No one had crossed the river in living memory, because, on the bridge that crossed the wild water, there lay a most fearsome dragon.

It was serpentine, long, coiled on itself, and huge. It had been sleeping for two thousand years and, in all that time, no one had dared walked across the water. However, Hidesato longed to go to the other side, as he was a most curious young man. His bravery and desire for learning run deeper than whatever fear a dragon could cause, so he began to walk across the bridge.

Despite being careful, Hidesato stepped on one of the creature's whiskers and, with a flurry of scales, the immense being rose, twirled, roared… and then sank into the river, leaving the boy intact.

Too stunned for words, he did not move until a maiden, dripping with silver droplets and bathed in light, rose from the water. Standing before the flabbergasted Hidesato, she said with a laughing voice, 'Brave man, at last, you've come! I have been waiting for one such as you for many a year. I have a perilous enemy, you see, the venomous Ōmukade centipede, and I can only trust to be my champion someone who is not afraid to face me.' Awed, Hidesato agreed to face Ōmukade on her behalf and, donning his family arms, set out.

Being our hero, he (of course) defeated the terrible monster on top of Mount Mikami. He fired three fiery arrows directly into the centipede's bright eyes and vanquished it forever, keeping his word to the Dragon Maiden.

When he came back, bathed in glory and a little worse for wear, she was waiting for him at the bridge. 'You have saved me!' she exclaimed and, filled with gratitude, dived with him into the river. Hidesato was surprised: he could breathe underwater! Looking into the Dragon Maiden's eyes, he understood it was her magic that protected him, just as he had protected her.

Swimming in dragon form, she took him to the Underwater Castle and, once there, she changed back into human form and regaled him with the most delicious food and music Hidesato had ever heard.

Tales of Dragons

As a reward for his exemplary faithfulness, virtue, and courage, she gave the young warrior five gifts: a temple bell, dragon-forged armor, a magic sword, a piece of silk that would last forever, and a bag of rice that would never run out, no matter how many people ate from it nor for how long.

Hidesato returned to the surface world carrying these precious treasures and the blessing from the Dragon Maiden. He went on to become a great warrior and a prosperous, beloved chieftain. In honour of his courageous adventure and the generosity he showed with his gifts, everyone called him 'My Lord Bag of Rice'.

THE CUELEBRE OF PEÑA URUEL

Spain

In the mountain of Uruel, near the fortified town of Jaca, there lived a dragon or, as the locals it terrorized called it, a cuelebre. It was a giant green serpent with enormous wings, sharp claws, and even sharper teeth. This was, to say the least, of a fiery nature — it used its incendiary breath to threaten the villagers and poor peasants into giving it all their livestock to eat and, when that ran out, started asking for the young children (those, it said, tasted best).

Everyone in the vicinity was horrified, but no one was daring enough to do anything about it. You see, there was something about this dragon that made it seemingly impossible to defeat: its gaze, besides being quite frightful in itself (as dragon teeth are very close to dragon eyes), was deadly. One glance and you're turned to stone! It is, then, understandable that no man nor valiant knight was brave enough to face the beast.

The devastation continued. That is, until one particular morning in which a young lad rode up to the mountain carrying a tin shield, and told everyone who would listen that he was going to take down the cuelebre. The villagers laughed — this boy was not known for his strength and, though very clever, they did not believe he could outmatch a dragon.

He smiled and said nothing, using what time he had before the dragon came to polish his flimsy tin shield so it shone like the sun. And the dragon came slithering down, not bothering to use its wings (it was nice and fat), making the ground shake.

The boy got ready — he didn't even have a sword! — and, when the monster was close, shouted a challenge and hid behind the tin shield. Lo and behold! Though it was no weapon, the shield was just polished enough that it reflected the deadly glare back at the cuelebre, killing it instantly! They were now safe and free!

Amidst disbelieving relief, the villagers carried the boy — now a hero — on their shoulders to the fortified town of Jaca, where he ate to his heart's content and did not have to go hungry ever again.

THE SEVEN-HEADED MANITOU

Canada (Ojibwe)

On a farm, there lived a poor man with his wife. They had no children. One day, desperate for food, the man went fishing and caught a very slippery trout. The animal said to him, 'Wait! I'll grant you a gift: do not throw away any of my scales, but bury them in your garden. Give your wife half of my body to eat, and the other half to the dog.' Of course, the man obeyed the talking fish. He told his wife about the strange instructions he'd received, and they did as they were told.

Can you imagine the surprise of these poor farmers when, by the next morning, all their animals, plants, and money had been doubled? They were not poor anymore! That night, the wife conceived and, as they found out nine moons later, they had a pair of healthy, strapping twins.

As they now had everything they needed, no one in the family went outside the bounds of their land. But, as growing lads are always curious, one of the twins asked their father, 'Are there other people in the world?'. 'Of course!' replied the father and realised, only too late, that this son would leave them and go travel to make his own fortune.

With tears, they let him go. He took with him the dog (who had eaten half of the fish body and was now magical), and they walked for days before finding anyone at all. But, finally, he saw a town all decked in black. It was deathly silent.

He approached the local blacksmith and asked why the town was mourning, and could he stay the night? 'Of course,' the man replied, 'And we are in mourning because all of our maidens have been devoured by the dragon Manitou who lives on the mountain, the dreadful Windigo. And, now that no others are left, even the beautiful chief's daughter will have to be sacrificed tomorrow'.

The young man pondered this and, as soon as the sun rose, set out for the mountain. He had, after all, nothing to lose. He was almost there when he saw a beautiful girl weeping, and an old marshal consoling her halfheartedly.

'What's wrong?' the lad asked. 'I'm being taken to the mountain to be eaten by the Windigo,' she replied sadly. 'It cannot be helped!' the marshal added, 'It's for the common good.'

The hero thought him cold and, with bravery in his voice, instructed the girl to stay put: he would deal with the Windigo himself. With a glimpse of hope in her lovely eyes, the chief's daughter gave him a ring and wished him luck.

Taking heart, he climbed the steep slopes and, when he reached the top, waited. Suddenly, he felt the earth tremble and the trees around him shake. The air grew hot, dense, and poisonous: the Manitou had arrived. With a roar, it appeared.

The monster one powerful, armored body and seven ghastly heads that thrashed, looking for a maiden to bite and devour. When the fourteen awful eyes found him and realised he was no the morsel they were expecting, the Windigo attacked.

The hero dashed this way and that, struggling to avoid the Manitou's many sharp fangs and claws until, finally, he cut one of the heads off. It grew again! Suddenly realizing what he had to do, the young man cut it off again and tossed it to his dog, telling him to hold onto it. With a great deal of effort, he managed to do the same with the remaining heads and, at last, the Manitou lay dead atop the mountain.

After cutting off the seven tongues of the dragon as a trophy and a gift for the girl's father, the lad descended to where the chief's daughter and the marshal waited and gave her the tongues.

Our hero was exhausted and, though he thought of resting on the ground for a little while, he fell into a deep sleep. The girl thought there was no harm in coming down without him — she would go first and announce him to his father.

But, on the way back, the old, cowardly marshal said, 'You will give me the tongues and tell your father it was I who killed the Manitou. If you refuse, I will kill you.' Afraid, the girl did as she was told and her father, pleased to see his daughter again, announced she and the marshal were to be married that very night — even though she did not want to.

When the wedding feast was going on, the hero — finally awake — walked in and immediately understood what had happened. When the girl saw him, she took her chance and told her father the truth of what had happened. 'He has my ring as proof that this is true,' she explained.

Ashamed to have been played for a fool, the chief walked up to the hero, who was sitting near the door and invited him to a place of honour. When the traitorous marshal saw this, he tried to escape but was caught. The chief declared him guilty and, with great applause from the crowd, he was thrown out onto the stormy sea in a little barge.

The hero, however, received great honour and married the chief's daughter who loved him, as he had saved her at his own risk. They were happy for many years and became powerful, prosperous, and famous.

THE DRAGON PRINCESS

China

In the Sea of Dungting, in the East there are a great many wondrous and mysterious things, and, among them, a bottomless hole. So what happened when a distracted, dirty, and lost fisherman fell in?

When he fell into the hole, he kept falling for a long time. But, eventually, he arrived at a country with green, rolling hills as well as very odd plants and animals he'd never before seen. Walking in amazement, he found himself before a great castle and directly in front of the snout of an enormous sea dragon. Wrinkling its face in distaste, the creature merely refused him entry but didn't harm him.

After some time of exploration, he found a way out and went directly to the Emperor. He told the court everything about this strange new land. The Emperor's wise man became very excited: he knew many things about the Dragon People of the Dungting Sea. For example, that they hated tree wax (the fisherman's clothes reeked of it, and so the dragons hadn't touched him). More importantly, he knew that every dragon has, at least, one magical pearl that it keeps under his chin.

But the Sea King's daughter, the Dragon Princess, whose castle the fisherman had seen, had a whole hoard of them tucked away. The wise man proposed that the Emperor should send his most courteous and worthy messengers, armed with a protective stone, to see the Dragon Princess. They would take a load of swallows (the Dragons' favourite meal) and dragon-brain vapour, which would compel their hosts to give them the treasure they sought.

Lo-Dsi-Tschun and his two brothers were chosen as envoys, as they were related to the Dragon King through a distant ancestor. After being wholly dunked in smelly tree wax (just a precaution, as dragons are always perilous), the brothers set out. They offered swallows to the guards, who devoured the food and, disliking the smell of the brothers, let them pass.

When they arrived at the castle, they were received by the Dragon Princess and her own wise counselor, a thousand-year-old dragon

who could turn into a human at will. He read the letter from the Emperor, which demanded a gift of magical pearls in exchange for a thousand delicious swallows.

The Princess smiled enigmatically. The brothers were treated courteously: they got the best fare of their lives— all flowers and fine herbs— and couldn't resist sneaking some into their saddlebags for the way home.

Eventually, thanks to the offerings done to her, the Princess consented, just for once, to give the Emperor the magical pearls he sought: a total of ten supernatural ones and innumerable common ones. The brothers, grateful not to have been eaten, bowed low. Their amazement was even greater when they were invited to ride to the surface on the back of a twisting, dancing dragon. They were sure that half the turns he took were only intended to make them feel dizzy and lost. Dragons like that sort of jokes.

Back at the court, the brothers handed the treasure to the Emperor and the whole court admired it, as well as their bravery and negotiating skills.

As for Lo-Dsi-Tschun and the other two travellers, they opened the bags to eat the rest of the marvelous food they had brought back only to discover that, in contact with the harsh air of our reality, it had become as hard as a stone!

The three brothers laughed and looked at each other with a light in their hearts. It did not matter that they got no prize for their dangerous journey. Sometimes, they had learnt, an adventure in which you meet creatures far greater than you knew before is, in itself, its own reward.

29649047R00029

Made in the USA
Lexington, KY
01 February 2019